# That's Not All!

Written and Illustrated by
## Rex Schneider

# What a way to start a day!

A mouse is in my house.

A bug has dug into my rug.

My pet goose
let the moose loose.

That's not all!
A goat is eating my coat.

A hen has my pen in the den.

My cat is in love with a rat.

My dog is being a hog.

That's not all!
That bat was in my hat.

The pig took my wig.

A clown took my gown.

A pink mink is in my sink.

And my sheep will not sleep.

There is a way to end this day.
I will run to join the fun!

Join us!